THE HONEYBEARS' CHRISTMAS SURPRISE

Written by R.C. Andrea
Illustrated by Yuri Salzman

"Wake up! Wake up!" said Dawn. "It's Christmas Eve, and we have lots to do today." So the Honeybears jumped out of bed, got dressed, and rushed downstairs to eat breakfast.

They ate plenty of buns covered with honey. Then
Checkers and Dawn, along with their friend Honeysuckle, the
Bee, went to find that special Christmas tree.

Meanwhile, Holly and Ralph unpacked the Christmas
decorations. They hung the stockings and began stringing
garlands of popcorn.

At Old Thor's Tree Farm, Checkers and Dawn searched and searched, but still could not find the right tree.

"Come quick! Come quick!" buzzed Honeysuckle. "I found it! I found it!" They ran to the farthest corner of the farm. There, all alone and forgotten, stood a small, perfect Christmas tree.

"That's my favorite tree," thundered Old Thor, "and it's not for sale!"

"Well sir, we've brought some honey," said Dawn. Old Thor's eyes lit up when he saw the golden honey pot. Before he knew it, the Honeybears and his favorite tree were on their way home.

On with the ornaments! Up with the stockings! Everyone
moved with excitement. At last the star was placed on top of
the tree and the Honeybears were ready for Christmas.

"Don't forget the cookies for Santa," shouted Ralph.
"Right. Now everything is perfect," said Holly, "except
that Cousin Eddie isn't here."

"Cousin Eddie," they all sighed. Their favorite cousin,
who always made them laugh, would not be here for
Christmas. He was in all their thoughts, as the bears went to bed.

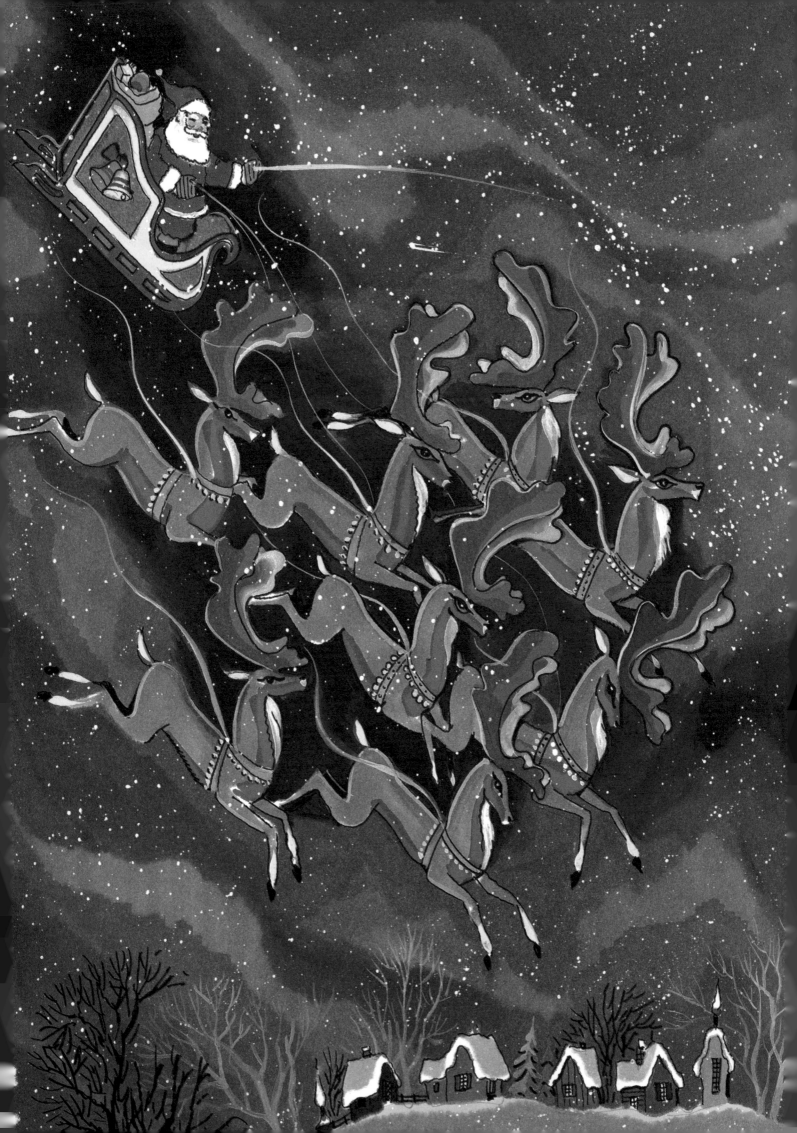

Soon the Honeybears were fast asleep. A soft jingle was heard in the air, as Santa landed with his reindeer and sleigh.

Down the chimney he went, with his bag full of toys for the Honeybear girls and the Honeybear boys.

Beneath the tree, Santa placed the presents. Then he filled each stocking, and taking a handful of cookies, he went on his merry way.

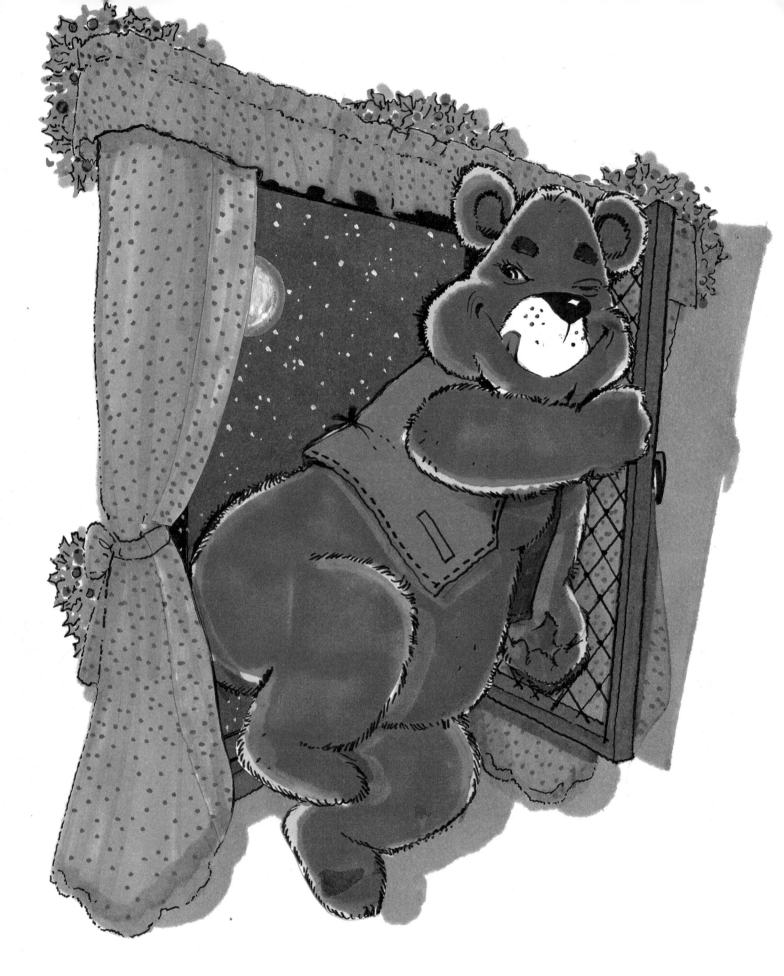

Not long after, a shadowy figure appeared. It quietly opened the window, and climbed into the room. Then with a wide grin, it slowly walked through the Christmasy house.

Early the next morning, Honeysuckle was the first to rise. "Merry Christmas! Merrry Christmas!" he cried. The Honeybears bounced out of bed and wished each other a Merry Christmas.

"I can't wait to open my presents," said Ralph. "Come on, let's go!" They all ran downstairs, and headed for the tree.

But, the floor beneath the Christmas tree was bare! The Honeybears rushed to their stockings, but they were . . . empty! The bears were heartbroken.

"Where are the presents?" asked Holly.
"I guess Santa forgot about us," replied Dawn. Tears began to fill their eyes.

Then suddenly a voice called out, "Santa didn't forget you. He *was* here last night, and so was I. SURPRISE!" Up from behind the couch jumped Cousin Eddie.

For a moment the Honeybears couldn't believe their eyes. Then they began to laugh and laugh. "You told us you couldn't be here for Christmas," said Checkers, as he hugged his cousin.

"Well, here I am. I just wanted to surprise you," said Eddie.

"I'm so happy to see you," cried Ralph.

"So am I. So am I," said Honeysuckle.

"If Santa had not forgotten our presents," added Dawn, "this would have been the best Christmas ever."

Cousin Eddie's face wore a familiar smile. Suddenly the bears realized that he had played one of his tricks on them. "I thought it might be lots of fun to have a Christmas present hunt," said Eddie.

And indeed it was. The Honeybears dashed through the house laughing and shouting. Toys and gifts were hidden everywhere.

Later, they gathered around the Christmas tree, and opened their presents. Cousin Eddie gave presents to Ralph, Checkers, Holly and Dawn. And of course, he had one for Honeysuckle too.

Then the warm glow of Christmas filled the room. The Honeybears all agreed with Holly when she said, "Cousin Eddie, you're the best Christmas present of all."